Jasmine's Lucky Star

"Is he coming to see you?"

I wasn't sure what Poppy meant. "Who?"

"Your dad. Is he coming to watch you in the show?"

My stomach was suddenly full of butterflies. "I hadn't even thought about that. I don't know... I suppose so..."

"Well that's good, isn't it?" said Poppy. "Because then he'll see how good you are and it might make him change his mind about the whole thing and say you're allowed to carry on with ballet lessons, even after primary school!"

Ballerina Dreams

Collect all the books in the series:

Poppy's Secret Wish
Rose's Big Decision

Coming soon:

Dancing Princess
Dancing with the Stars

Ballerina Dreams

Jasmine's Lucky Star

Ann Bryant

USBORNE

The publisher would like to thank Sara Matthews of
the Central School of Ballet for her assistance.

✳

First published in the UK in 2004 by Usborne Publishing Ltd,
Usborne House, 83-85 Saffron Hill, London EC1N 8RT, England.
www.usborne.com

Copyright © 2004 by Ann Bryant

The right of Ann Bryant to be identified as the author of this work has been asserted by
her in accordance with the Copyright, Designs and Patents Act, 1988.

Cover photograph by Ray Moller.
Illustrations by Tim Benton.
The name Usborne and the devices ♀ ⊕ are Trade Marks
of Usborne Publishing Ltd. All rights reserved.

A CPI catalogue record for this title is available
from the British Library.

ISBN   0 7460 6025 4

Printed in India.

JFM MJJASOND/06

1 Turning Point

Hi! I'm Jasmine. And right now I'm feeling very excited because my best friends, Poppy and Rose, are coming for a sleepover. In a way, I wish it was just Poppy coming, so we could get on with our dance. We're doing the choreography ourselves and it's important to make it really good because it's for the show at the end of term.

Poppy and I don't go to the same school, but we do ballet together every Tuesday and we often go to each other's houses. She'll be here in a minute, and Rose isn't coming till a bit later, so that gives us time to work on the dance. But maybe "work" isn't the right word, because ballet is our very favourite thing in the whole world...

"Jasmeen!"

That's my mum calling me from downstairs. She's French, so she speaks with a bit of an accent. I bet I know what she wants.

"I've done it, Maman!" I called back. (I've always called her "Maman". It's the French for "Mum".)

"I can't talk through the door, Jasmeen!"

I went out onto the landing and leaned over the banister. "I've finished it all, honestly."

"Good girl. Papa will be pleased." She broke into a smile and I broke into a shiver. That's the effect my dad has on me. He's away at a doctors' conference at the moment, and I know it's horrible of me, but I like it when he's away. You see, he's very strict – stricter than any of my friends' dads. Even worse than that, he doesn't approve of ballet. He thinks there are much more important things that I should be doing, like homework. I also have a tutor once a week so that's even more homework. Then there's my piano practice that my teacher expects me to do five times a week for at least twenty minutes each time. It gets on my nerves. All I want to do is ballet!

When I'm eleven, Papa says that I'm going to a school called Mansons where the work's really hard. Rose's brother knows someone who goes there and he says you have to take loads of exams and pass them with very high marks and finish up by being a lawyer or a banker or a doctor or a big-chief executive or something.

And that's the problem. I don't want to be any of those things. All I want to be is a ballerina. Papa doesn't know that and, believe me, I'd never *ever* dare tell him. If he knew, he'd go mad and probably make me give up ballet lessons straight away. He wasn't very happy when it was my ballet exam and I had to have a few extra lessons last term. At the moment, I only have one lesson a week. He doesn't mind that because it doesn't interfere with my homework or the extra work that my tutor gives me, or my piano practice or anything. He doesn't realize how much time I spend practising ballet up in my room.

The worst thing of all is that Papa says I've got to give up ballet when I leave primary school. I used to think that was ages and ages away and that he'd have changed his mind by then, but I'm ten now and I'm scared that time's running out.

Rose is always saying that one of these days she's going to tell my dad a thing or two. I haven't known Rose as long as I've known Poppy, so she's never actually met Papa. Poppy and I have both tried to explain that he's not the kind of dad that you go round "telling a thing or two" to, but Rose doesn't really get how strict he is.

"Poppy will be here in a few minutes, chérie," called Maman. "Is your room tidy?"

I sighed. "Yes, my homework's done and my room's tidy."

"Oh, there she is now!" Maman turned at the sound of the doorbell.

"It's okay, I'll get it." I shot downstairs and got to the door just before her.

Poppy was standing on the doorstep with her bag, her hair already scraped back in a bun, her ballet hairband on and a big smile on her face. "Hi, Jasmine! Look!" She yanked the poppers on her denim jacket apart. "I'm ready, see! I've got my tights on under my jeans."

Then my mum came into view and Poppy went pink. She often goes pink. She's got the kind of skin that shows it easily – very fair with freckles, to go with her lovely auburn hair.

"Hello, Poppy. Lovely to see you!" Behind her in the car, I could see Poppy's mum smiling and waving.

"I'll have a quick word..." said Maman, patting Poppy on the shoulder as she went past, "...see what time your mum wants to collect you tomorrow."

"As late as possible!" I called out, dragging Poppy inside. "Come on, let's go up to my room."

As soon as we closed the bedroom door behind us, Poppy bounced on my bed and shrugged the backpack off her shoulders. "I'm so excited. We've got ages, haven't we? I really want Miss Coralie to be pleased when she sees all our hard work on Tuesday. How much of the dance have you made up so far?"

I was getting changed, smoothing my tights and putting my leotard on. "The *whole* dance! It's because I love the music so much. I can't wait to show you."

Poppy jumped up. Her eyes were shining. "I think we chose the *best* music. I'm so glad we were all allowed to take the tape of our dance home."

"Which is your favourite bit?"

"Probably the tinkly high bit...or maybe the ending...or that shimmery sliding part..." Poppy lay back on my bed and started doing scissor legs. "It was incredible when Miss Coralie said that we could choreograph our own dances for the show, wasn't it? Thank goodness I've got you for my partner. You're so much better than me at working out which steps go together to make the best choreography." She drew her knees up and hugged them tight.

I was standing in front of my mirror, doing my hair, but Poppy's words took me right back to Tuesday's lesson. When I looked at my reflection, all I could see was a picture of Miss Coralie's face, her eyes flashing round our silent group as she'd told us about the show.

"This is a ballet school with a reputation for a very high standard of dance, so I want to see some serious work going on. Then we'll have a

professional, high-quality show that we can all be proud of."

I concentrated on gripping my ponytail tight, trying not to let a single hair move out of place as I looped the band, so there would be no trace of any bumps. But I was so used to doing this that my hands could manage it without any help from my brain. That meant my mind could go off where it wanted. Miss Coralie's no-nonsense look appeared in front of my eyes again.

"The show is to be called 'Shades of Nature' and it's in three sections. The first one is for all the younger pupils. They are doing dances based on animals, birds and flowers. The older girls are going to be working in three groups, representing earth, fire and water..." The silence had been so deep at that moment that you could have heard a flower opening. I remember how Miss Coralie's eyes had moved slowly over us.

"*Your class, and the one that comes before you on Tuesdays, will make up the middle section of the show. You will dance the sky, the moon...the stars, the sun...or any kind of weather – snow, frost, mist...*" Her hands had been floating in graceful looping movements as she'd given us the list, but then they'd suddenly stopped in midair for her next words. "*And I shall not be doing the choreography. YOU will!*" There'd been quite a gasp when she'd said that, like a sparkler whooshing into life, but then dying down to a quieter crackling excitement when Miss Coralie went on to explain that we had to work in groups of two, three or four. "*I don't think you should form larger groups than this, because you'll need to get together to do a bit of extra practice between lessons...*"

The moment I'd heard the word *extra*, my heart had started racing away. Just remembering it sent a shiver right through me now as I pushed my hairband into place. It turned out that Miss Coralie had only meant extra practice at home, not extra proper rehearsals or anything, but my very first thought had been: *"Oh, no! Papa won't let me do any extra. What if I'm not allowed in the show?"*

"What are you thinking about, Jazz?"

Poppy's voice made me jump. "Nothing much."

"Bet it was your dad."

She was standing just behind me now. I smiled at her in the mirror. "You're good at reading minds, Poppy."

"You always wear that look when you're worrying about your dad. What's he done now?"

"Nothing. I was just imagining how terrible it would have been if there'd been extra rehearsals for the show and he'd said I wasn't allowed to go."

Poppy put her hands on her waist and heaved

a big sigh, pretending to be exasperated with me. "Well there *aren't* any, so you don't have to worry, do you?"

I didn't reply, just went over to my tape recorder and started rewinding the tape.

"Is he coming to see you?"

I wasn't sure what Poppy meant. "Who?"

"Your dad. Is he coming to watch you in the show?"

My stomach was suddenly full of butterflies. "I hadn't even thought about that. I don't know... I suppose so..."

"Well that's good, isn't it?" said Poppy. "Because then he'll see how good you are and it might make him change his mind about the whole thing and say you're allowed to carry on with ballet lessons, even after primary school!"

My heart nearly stopped when she said that. "But what if he thinks I'm complete rubbish and says I've got to finish at the end of term?"

"Don't be silly, Jazz. You're the best. We're the

youngest in the class *and* only you and Tamsyn got honours for grade four. That proves it!"

I turned round and looked at Poppy. Her eyes were dancing and her hands were clasped together as though she'd just heard that she'd been accepted into the Royal Ballet. "This could be a big important moment in your life, Jazz. When did your dad last see you dancing on a stage?"

I thought back. It seemed an awfully long time ago. "Well, he couldn't come last year because he was away on business. And the year before that...oh, yes, he had to do an emergency operation... Erm...I think it must have been three years ago."

Poppy jumped up, grabbed one of my hands and squeezed it tight. "You were only little then. He's no idea how good you are *now*, Jazz. You'll give him a real big shock!" Her eyes sparkled. "Just imagine, he'll be sitting in the audience expecting to see you come on in a little frilly tutu and start twizzling round with your hands above your head, looking like you did the last time he saw you. Then he'll sit up straighter than straight and stare his head off, because you'll be so brilliant he won't believe it!" Poppy suddenly gave me her most serious look and spoke in a slow, grave voice. "So it's very important, Jazz, that you do your best-ever choreography and your very-best-ever dancing. It'll be more than just a dance. It'll be a...a turning point in your life. Your dad will realize he *can't* stop such a talent and he's *got* to agree to let you carry on for ever!"

Goose bumps started to come up all over my arms. The nice, shivery, magicky sort of goose bumps. Poppy was slowly breaking into a smile. It was as though her happiness was seeping through her hands into mine. It might be possible. It just might. And if I *could* make it happen, it would be the best thing that had ever *ever* happened to me.

The moment I'd had that thought, every drop of happiness dissolved into thin air. "But Papa knows what grade I'm on. He said, 'Well done,' loads of times when I got honours for the exam."

"That's not the same," said Poppy firmly. "My parents both said well done when I got a merit, but they don't have a clue what that means. They don't know how much progress I've made. They never get to see us dance properly, do they?"

I sighed a long slow sigh. "Do you really think I could make him change his mind, Poppy?"

For answer, Poppy pressed her thumb against mine. It's our special good luck signal. We call it a thumb-thumb. And this time I knew I was going to need luck more than ever.

2 Starshine

"What time's Rose coming?" asked Poppy, her hand on the back of my chair. She was using it as a *barre* to hold on to while she did some *pliés* to warm up.

"Oh, no! She'll be here in an hour," I said, looking at my watch.

The moment I'd spoken, I felt a bit embarrassed. It sounded like I didn't want Rose here. When I'm embarrassed, I don't go red like Poppy, I just feel all hot, because redness doesn't show up on my olive skin. My dad's Egyptian, so that's where I get my dark skin from.

"Let's get on with it, quick," said Poppy. "We need to do as much as possible before she gets here."

I felt better knowing that Poppy agreed with me about that. You see, Rose has only been doing ballet for just over a term. She really hated it when she first started, and she doesn't exactly love it now, but at least she doesn't hate it any more. All the same, I *know* Rose, and so I said, "She'll get bored really quickly watching us, won't she?"

"Maybe she could pretend to be one of those critics from the newspaper who writes about ballets they've seen?" suggested Poppy, looking a bit doubtful.

I tried to imagine Rose sitting down and writing about me and Poppy practising. "I suppose she could tell us which bits are good and which are rubbish..."

"None of it will be rubbish," said Poppy. "*Will* it?" she added, giving me a pretend stern look to check that I'd remembered about making this dance the best ever.

A little shiver went through me again. "Right, let's get started." I went over to the tape recorder.

"Oh, hang on a sec," said Poppy, rootling round in her backpack. "I made up a poem to go with the dance, and I was wondering if we could record it onto a cassette and play it to the audience before the music started..." She suddenly went pink again. "I mean, only if you like the poem...I've called it 'Starshine'."

I took the piece of paper that she was holding out and started reading. I'm normally a fast reader, but the words of Poppy's poem made me slow down. "It's brilliant, Poppy. You're so clever. We'll show it to Miss Coralie on Tuesday!" Then I had an even better idea. "Why don't we call our dance *Starshine* too?"

Poppy smiled happily and sat up straight on the bed. "Okay, show me what you've worked out."

"Right, I'll try to explain at the same time. We start in opposite corners at the back... If this is the stage and that's the audience, I'll be here and you'll be there..." I said, putting the music on, "...and we'll run forward on tiptoe, and finish in this position, only you'll be facing this way. And this fast bit goes like this..." I started doing the repeated sequence of *pas de bourrées* and *jetés* that I'd worked out, but it suddenly seemed too easy. I was sure I could make it better... "Actually we ought to have *sissonnes* and *echappés* in here as well...yeah, and we could do it in a round!" Poppy was looking a bit puzzled, but I knew she easily understood all the French names of the steps, and she'd soon pick up how to do it, so I just carried on.

"This part will be me doing that *pas de bourrée* step I showed you near the beginning, and you'll be doing it to the other side, only with your arms in second..." I was imagining my dad in the audience. Oh, dear. It wasn't going to be good enough. "Maybe we could do some *fouettés* here...I know we've never learned them, but I think I can do them...and then suddenly go into an *arabesque* with arms like this."

The more I talked, the more Poppy's eyebrows began to draw together, until they were practically joined up she was wearing such a massive frown.

"I'm not sure I'll be able to do all this, Jazz..."

"You'll be fine, Poppy, honestly. Look..." I showed her a little sequence of *temps levé, chassé, pas de bourrée*, into fourth, and *pirouette*. "See," I said in an even more puffed-out voice, "and you could do it on the opposite leg to the opposite corner so we're mirroring each other..."

"Can you just slow down a bit, Jazz...?"

The trouble was, I couldn't slow down. I'd got so many ideas in my head now and I kept wanting to change things to make the dance better and better. It had to be perfect, absolutely perfect. Then Papa would think I was talented, and he might let me carry on.

But suddenly a loud silence hit the room. Poppy had gone over to the tape recorder and pressed the stop button. Her shoulders were slumped forwards and, when she spoke, her voice was not much more than a whisper. "I'll never pick it up like this, Jazz. I'm not as good as you..."

I clapped my hand to my mouth, feeling terrible. I didn't know what had got into me. "Yes, you *are*. It's totally my fault." I gave her a hug. "I shouldn't keep changing it all the time."

Poppy sat on the bed. "Why don't I just sit here watching, and you tell me when you're double positive that you're not going to change it any more?"

"No, it's okay. I'm going right back to what I

made up before. Come on, let's start at the very beginning, and this time I *promise* not to change anything."

So that's what we did and, about an hour later, Poppy had learned the whole dance. She'd written it all down too so she could practise at home.

"It's so cool, Jazz!" she kept on saying. "I can't wait to show Miss Coralie on Tuesday. I'm going to do so much practice that I'll be able to do it standing on my head by then!"

I tried to be happy too. I really did, but there was a little voice nagging away at me, telling me that the dance could still be better. *Should* be better. The inside of my body was full of sighs, but I didn't let them show on the outside, because poor Poppy would be completely fed up if I tried to start changing things again now. And, anyway, Rose would be here any minute.

"Hiya, folks!"

And there she was – bang on cue! – standing in the doorway wearing a pair of jeans that looked very old and tatty and a bit too big for her. I expect they used to belong to one of her brothers. Rose has got three big brothers and she often wears hand-me-downs, as she calls them. She doesn't care at all. In fact, I don't think she'd care if she was wearing a pair of her dad's pyjamas.

"Your mum let me in. I heard the music when I was in the hall. It sounds really great." She dropped her bag on the floor and nudged it into the corner with her foot. "Show me how it goes then!"

I really did not feel like showing Rose our dance, because I knew it would only make me want to start changing things again. "We'll show you when we've finished it, okay?"

"Oh, come on, Jazz! I've been dying to see it. I can help you if you're stuck for ideas." Poppy gave me an anxious look and Rose immediately burst out laughing. "Only kidding! You should see the look on your faces!"

So then we were all laughing.

"Right, I'm ready!" Rose said, springing on the bed and sitting up perfectly straight. "Hit it!"

I still didn't feel like going through it again though. Poppy didn't look exactly keen either. All the same, she'd got into her starting position, so I went over to the tape recorder. But when I turned round, Rose was standing up with Poppy's poem in her hand. "Hey! Cool!" she breathed. "Where did you get this from?"

"Poppy made it up," I told her.

"Wow! You could have it at the beginning of your dance, you know! Then the audience would get what the dance was all about."

"That's what *we* thought," said Poppy, turning all pink again. "We're going to ask Miss..."

But Rose was reading out loud as though she was performing on television.

The sky is deep and dark.
The sky is dark and deep.
The world is still and silent.
Everyone's asleep...

As she carried on reading, the poem came to life. And by the time she'd finished, I'd had the most brilliant idea. "Why doesn't Rose stand on the stage at the very beginning of our dance and read the poem out loud to the audience!"

Poppy's eyes sparkled as she looked at Rose. "Yes, that would be perfect," she squeaked, "because we'd all be in the dance then...in a way."

Rose shook her head slowly and broke into a big smile. "I just knew you couldn't do without me."

So, for the second time since she'd arrived, we were all in fits of laughter.

3 Filling up the Music

The sleepover was brilliant. First we all tried to squash into my bed, but it didn't really work because of Rose wriggling all the time. So Poppy slept in my bed and Rose and I had sleeping-bag beds on the floor. Even then, we couldn't get to sleep because Rose kept complaining that her sleeping bag was too girlie. In the end I let her have my dark blue one, and I had the one covered in pink teddy bears.

The last thing I remember before I went to sleep was Rose telling jokes that she'd got from her brothers. In the morning, she told us that she was right in the middle of one when she suddenly realized that Poppy and I were both fast asleep. At breakfast time, we asked her to tell us the joke again, but she was too busy eating.

"I love croissants," she said, spitting bits of puff pastry out of her mouth by mistake. "Whoops. Sorry!"

Maman laughed. "Me too," she said. "They make me think of breakfast at home when I was a little girl."

Rose licked the end of her finger and pressed it onto a flake of croissant on her plate, then popped it in her mouth, grinning at Maman. "Waste not, want not. That's what *my* mum's always saying."

Poppy smiled a bit nervously because she's much shyer in front of people's parents than Rose is. I'm fine with anyone's parents. Except my own dad...

Rose dabbed every single little flake of

croissant from her finger into her mouth, one at a time. She seemed to take for ever... The very second she'd finished, I asked Maman if we could leave the table.

"Yes, if you've all had enough. What are you going to do this morning?"

"Practise our dance," I said quickly.

Rose was not impressed. She pretended to go cross-eyed. "Are there any more croissants?"

Maman laughed. "I don't know where you put it all!"

So, while Rose carried on eating, Poppy and I went upstairs to practise. But, from the moment we started dancing, my legs felt like lead because I'd got that feeling again. And this time it was too big to ignore. I just knew that there was more in the music than there was in our dance. And I also knew that I'd never be happy until I'd made it perfect.

Maybe if I made just a teeny change to start with. "Try this, Poppy..."

"Oh, no... Not again, Jazz! I was just getting good at it yesterday. Please don't say you want to change it."

"Only a bit, honestly."

I tried to stop after the first change, but I couldn't because more and more ideas were tumbling out. *Sissonne en avant, sissonne en arrière, sissonne en avant, soubresaut, soubresaut,* and all the time arms changing position. When I finally looked up, Rose was standing beside Poppy. I hadn't even heard her come in.

"Isn't Poppy *in* this bit then, Jazz?"

I felt guilty when she said that. And selfish too.

"It's okay," said Poppy quietly to Rose. "It's just that Jazz is trying to make it as perfect as possible for her dad."

"For her *dad*! Why? He doesn't even *like* ballet!"

I had to admit that it seemed weird when Rose put it like that. But she didn't understand.

Poppy tried to explain. "You see, Jazz and I think that if her dad comes to watch the show and he sees how talented she is, he might let her carry on with ballet after all."

Rose rolled her eyes. "Huh! Very kind of him, I'm sure! You're already brilliant, Jazz. You shouldn't have to prove that to your dad, you know!"

I was starting to feel cross. The trouble was, in my heart I knew that Rose was right. But she didn't realize about Papa. He really *would* stop me doing lessons at the end of primary, unless I somehow managed to make him change his mind. I heaved a big sigh and hung my head. I was fed up with thinking about it all the time. Immediately, Rose shot across the room and gave me a tight hug. "Don't worry, Jazz. Just wait till he gets back from his conference. I'm going to tell him a thing or two, you'll see!"

My heart did a backflip.

"You can't talk to him, Rose," said Poppy, looking anxious. "You'll make him cross."

"What time's he coming home?" asked Rose.

"Not till after you've gone," I quickly said (which was true).

"Maybe I'll leave him a note," said Rose, looking thoughtful. But, a second later, she'd broken into her usual grin. "Only joking!"

Rose had to go home after lunch, so Poppy and I spent more time working on the dance.

"Miss Coralie won't believe her eyes, Jazz. She'll be really pleased with your choreography," said Poppy.

I pretended to agree, but still the little voice inside my head kept jabbing away at my brain. *It's not good enough. It's not good enough. It could be better. It could be better.*

Poppy's mum came to pick Poppy up just after that and, while our mums were talking, we did a quick thumb-thumb.

"Hope Miss Coralie lets Rose say the poem," whispered Poppy.

I nodded, but I wasn't thinking about that.

After they'd gone, I went back up to my room and got my bag ready for school the next day. Then I sat on the floor and listened to the *Starshine* music with my eyes closed. I went through the steps in my head, trying to picture myself with Poppy, performing our dance on the lovely big stage at the new Community Centre Hall. I concentrated hard right up to the final position and then I imagined the clapping. When it finished I stayed perfectly still with my eyes closed, wondering why I felt so empty.

I got up slowly and rewound the tape. I didn't press play straight away. Instead I stood at the window and looked at the sky. The bluey-grey was beginning to turn dark and smudged. I felt sure that what I could see was only the first layer of sky and that there would be more and more layers, each one a shade deeper than the last.

> *The sky is deep and dark.*
> *The sky is dark and deep.*
> *The world is still and silent.*
> *Everyone's asleep...*

Without taking my eyes off the sky, I felt behind me for the play button on the tape recorder and pressed it. As I stared into the distance, I imagined two glinting stars, weaving and crisscrossing, zipping and spinning. And every loop, every swirl and twirl left the finest trail of glittering silver dust behind it. My head was filled with the magic of the dance and I could see the steps I wanted, completely clearly now. I rushed to get my note pad so I could write them all down.

For the next few minutes, there was not a sound in my room. Yet, inside my head, the music was playing loudly and clearly.

I put the tape back on and danced the new steps through, imagining Poppy's part at the same time. At last, the dance had come alive. It all worked perfectly. I rewound the tape and tried it once more, but this time I heard something else above the sound of the music. It was Rose's words inside my head. They seemed to be mocking me.

"You're already brilliant, Jazz. You shouldn't have to prove that to your dad, you know."

"That's it!" I suddenly blurted out to the empty room. I could feel a kind of strength pushing its way out from my brain, right to my fingertips and the ends of my toes. I'd realized something important. I'd made the dance as good as I could make it. I'd done my very very best. I'd done it for Papa. So he could see me doing my very best. But it wasn't just for Papa. It was also for *me*.

I sat down on the bed feeling happy. Thank

goodness I'd decided to play through the music again. Thank goodness I'd managed to empty my mind of the old steps and let the music fill it up with the new ones. All I had to do now was to teach Poppy. She wasn't going to be very pleased when I told her that I'd changed it again, and it would be much more difficult to learn this new version, but once she'd learned it, I felt sure she'd realize how much better it was.

I went straight down to Maman and asked her if it would be okay for Poppy to come to tea the next day after school. She was a bit doubtful at first, but when I explained how important it was, she said I could phone.

"Hi, Poppy! Guess what!" I didn't wait for her to guess. "I've changed the dance. Only don't worry, it's…"

"Oh, Jazz… You shouldn't have done. Your dad will be impressed with what we've done already…"

"No, that's just it, Poppy. I've changed it because *I* wanted to make it better. I've done it for me."

Poppy didn't say anything. She obviously wasn't convinced. So I started gabbling. "It's a trillion times better than it was and I just know you're going to love it when I show you it and Miss Coralie will be much more pleased than she would have been."

"But we won't be able to show her, because I won't have learned it!"

"That's what I'm phoning about. Can you come to my house for tea tomorrow?"

A big sigh came down the line. "Hang on a sec. I'll just ask Mum."

I could hear Poppy and her mum talking and talking, and I could feel my spirits sinking at the same time because it sounded as though Poppy's mum had arranged something different.

I was right. "Sorry, Jazz. Mum says I can't because the hairdresser's coming. She's doing me and Stevie *and* Mum, so she won't be able to drive me over, you see."

Maybe there was a glimmer of hope. "Well, I could come to your house instead."

"That's what I just said to Mum, but she said no. I asked if I could go to ballet early on Tuesday though, and she said that's fine."

That was something, at least. I'd just have to learn my new choreography until I knew it backwards, then teach Poppy as much as possible before class. When I put the phone down I raced back upstairs to listen to the music again. I marked through the new steps, and suddenly I was imagining Papa in the audience. And then something hit me. What if Papa *wasn't* in the audience? What if he was away on business again? Would it be enough that I'd be dancing for myself? No, that was still only part of it. I *needed* Papa there to see what I could do.

I raced down to the kitchen, gabbling away

before I'd even got through the door.

"Maman...do you know if Papa's away on the twenty-seventh...?"

I stopped and stared.

"Ask him yourself, Jasmeen," said Maman with a smile.

I gulped. "I didn't know you were back, Papa."

"I've only just walked in!" he said, also smiling. But he looked tired as he patted my shoulder and gave me a kiss. "What's that music you're playing up there?"

"It's for the show. On the twenty-seventh. Will you be able to come?"

He flopped into a chair and closed his eyes for a moment.

"Let me make you a cup of tea," said Maman, flicking the switch on the kettle. "Your father's tired, Jasmeen."

"Yes, but can you just look in your diary, Papa?"

"What's the hurry, Jasmeen? Let your father have five minutes' peace."

I really wished Maman would stop interrupting. It was probably silly of me to keep going on about it, but I was so desperate to know. I spoke as quietly as possible, because it didn't seem so bad then. "Could you just look, Papa?"

He sighed and reached into his pocket for his electronic diary. Maman looked tense. I kept my eyes on Papa as he tapped the screen. "The twenty-seventh, you say?"

"Yes," I managed to croak.

"Looks all right. What time?"

My spirits soared. "Two thirty."

"Oh..." He frowned. My spirits sank. "Well, it depends. I'm away the previous night, but I *should* be back in time. I might miss the first part."

"Lovely," said Maman, cutting in briskly. "Can you get a cup and saucer out, Jasmeen?"

I did as I was told without saying anything else. There was no point. I couldn't change anything. It just meant that I'd be even more nervous on the day, because of wanting to do my best and also because of wondering whether Papa was in the audience or not.

4 Miss Coralie Means Business

All through school on Tuesday I was dying for the end-of-school bell to ring. It was impossible to concentrate on anything because my mind was full of the dance. I was desperate to start teaching it to Poppy.

It was such a relief when we actually met up in the changing room. But I couldn't help feeling disappointed to see that Tamsyn and a few others had got there early too, so they could go through their choreography.

"I think Room Two is free," I whispered to Poppy when we were bending over to put our shoes on.

"Have you two worked out your whole dance?" asked Tamsyn loudly.

"Jasmine's going to teach me now..." Poppy started to explain.

Tamsyn wrinkled her nose as though we'd made a bad smell come into the room. "You mean you haven't even tried it out together yet?"

I opened my mouth to answer, but she was already talking again. "Me and Immy and Lottie have made up a really brilliant dance. We spent nearly all Saturday doing it, didn't we, Immy?" Immy was eating crisps and concentrating on peering over Lottie's shoulder to read her magazine, so she didn't even hear. "We're doing an ice dance. Can you imagine how it looks – all that melting and freezing? I'm so glad I thought up that idea. I just know Miss Coralie's going to love it." Then she suddenly stood up and began to slide into the sideways splits, dropping her head back dramatically. "See. Good, isn't it?"

"Yeah, brill!" I spoke in a whisper to Poppy. "Let's go into the other room. No one's in there."

Tamsyn was getting into another ice-statue shape when we crept out.

"Right, we start in the same positions as before and we do the running on tiptoe, only you start four beats after me," I said to Poppy, "and we finish a bit further out than before…"

She nodded and we tried it, but it was hard to do with counts instead of music.

"Oh!" Tamsyn was standing in the doorway. "So that's where you got to! You had the same idea as us. We thought we'd have a run-through of ours too!" She started to come into the room. Immy and Lottie were in the doorway now.

Poppy bit her lip but she didn't say anything. It was up to me.

"Well actually, the thing is, Tamsyn… Do you mind trying yours out in the corridor? It's just that we've started all over again and we haven't had time to try it out together yet."

"But the corridor isn't big enough," said Tamsyn.

"It doesn't matter, Tams," said Lottie from the doorway. "Let Jazz and Poppy have this room."

"We've had loads of time to practise," Immy added.

Tamsyn didn't have any choice, because the other two had gone back to the changing room, but she didn't look too happy. "It's not my fault if you two haven't bothered to practise together..." she muttered as she went out.

Poppy tried calling after her. "We have, only..."

"Never mind about Tamsyn," I said. "Let's just get on."

And we tried. I knew it was best to start at the beginning, but unfortunately that was one of the most complicated bits. After the tiptoe running, we had to stay perfectly still. This was the moment the two stars realized that they were alone in the dark sky. Then they suddenly had to burst into action as though the search for each other had begun. The sequence I'd worked out for that bit was tricky for Poppy to learn, and she still hadn't got it when we heard the révérence music coming from Room One.

"We'll have to line up, Poppy. Our class will be starting in a minute."

"Can't we show Miss Coralie the old version, Jazz?"

"Don't worry, I'll explain..."

I was sounding brave, but inside I was as nervous as anything.

Everyone always stands up very straight when we're in the line waiting to go in. It's impossible to describe the feeling I get inside my chest when the door opens and the class before comes out. You see them go running lightly past, looking hot and tired and not saying a word to each other. And I always feel as if my heart's grown bigger.

I raised my eyebrows at Rose as she came out, which was my way of asking if she'd had a good lesson. She nodded and whispered to Poppy and me as she passed us. "My group's supposed to be doing a summer breeze, only they're complaining that I'm making it a hurricane!" Then she turned her palms up and pulled a face as though she didn't understand why they should say that.

"Come in, next class!" came Miss Coralie's firm voice.

Automatically I did what Miss Eleanor, my very first ballet teacher, taught me to do. I imagined I was a puppet, with the puppet master gently pulling on a thin piece of string that went in through the middle of the top of my head right inside me, down to my stomach. As the puppet master pulled, every bit of me rose up out of my abdomen in the straightest line.

Miss Coralie, all in black, apart from a beautiful pale green cross-over that matched her earrings, was standing in third position, watching us like a hawk as we ran with the lightest footsteps to the *barre*.

She waited till we were in fifth position, then said, "Good afternoon girls. Just a quick warm-up today because I'd like to see how your dances are developing. I shall be coming round from group to group. Right..." We waited for the magic words, as Mrs. Marsden, the pianist, lifted her hands ready to play the *plié* music. "*Preparation*...and..."

I love *pliés*. I don't know if it's because they're the very first thing we do at the beginning of class or because I just love them anyway.

"Nice, Jasmine," said Miss Coralie as she walked past me.

It's the most brilliant feeling when you get a "nice" or a "good" from Miss Coralie because she's got very high standards. In fact, she used to dance with the Royal Ballet Company. So if you get a "lovely" you feel over the moon.

After we'd done *battements tendus*, and some *grands battements*, Miss Coralie asked us to get into our groups and start work.

"I know it's not the same without music," she said, "but you can work on technique and expression. If there's time at the end, we might see one or two groups with the music. I trust everyone has practised since last Tuesday?" Miss Coralie's eyes passed over the groups. Poppy's elbow nudged my arm. I think she wanted me to say something. But it wasn't our turn. "Rainbow group, did you manage to get together?"

There were seven girls in one of the groups. Although Miss Coralie had said it would be best to be in small groups to make it easier to get together between lessons, she'd been so impressed with the idea of the rainbow that she'd allowed the group to be a seven.

The girls all nodded and one of them said they'd managed to work out the whole dance.

"That's what I like to hear," said Miss Coralie. She gave them a small smile as though she hadn't time for a big one, then moved on to Tamsyn's group.

"We've done all of ours, too," said Tamsyn in her usual loud voice.

"Excellent," said Miss Coralie with the same half-smile. "Alexandra and Becky, how is your story of the argument between the wind and the sun going?"

"We've sorted most of it out," said Alexandra, "but Becky's been off school most of the week."

Now it was nearly our turn my mouth was getting dry. I'd thought it was going to be so easy to explain about starting all over again, but Miss Coralie didn't seem in the right mood for listening to explanations.

"Glad you're better, Becky. And the girls doing the star dance? Jasmine? Poppy?"

Poppy was nudging me. I swallowed.

"Is there a problem, you two?"

"No... We've done it all," Poppy blurted out.

"Good, let's set to work then," said Miss Coralie. Then off she went to the rainbow group.

I swallowed again and looked at Poppy. Her freckles hardly showed at all because redness was hiding them. I felt sorry for her, but I was determined not to go back to the old dance.

"I'll never be able to do that new bit, Jazz. And then there's all the rest to learn."

"You'll be fine. Come on..."

We went over the first complicated sequence again, but Poppy was too nervous to concentrate. "It would be easier if we had the music," she said, biting her lip.

"I'll try and sing it, shall I?"

But we'd hardly started when Tamsyn's voice came ringing out. "Jasmine, can you be quiet, you're putting me off!" And Miss Coralie gave me a frown from across the room.

Quarter of an hour later, I felt much better. Poppy could do the sequence really well and we'd gone on to the next bit.

"Are you sure it's all right?" asked Poppy. "It doesn't feel as flowing as the last version."

"That's only because we haven't got the music and we haven't practised enough together," I told her.

Then Miss Coralie was suddenly at our side.

"Right, girls, from the top."

I really wanted to explain about how we'd made up the whole dance then completely changed it, but it was obvious from Miss Coralie's flashing eyes that she was in a big hurry, and didn't have time for talking. So we started.

Poppy was still nervous but she managed to get through the tricky bit and we also did the next part. It all seemed to be over in a flash.

"What about the rest of the dance?" asked Miss Coralie.

"Well, you see, we'd already made up the whole dance," Poppy started gabbling, "but then

Jasmine decided to change it..."

Miss Coralie turned her head sharply to look at me. "Change it?"

"To make it better," I said, feeling my cheeks going hot. "I've worked it out right to the end, only we didn't have time..."

Miss Coralie's eyes flickered over to the clock above the piano. "Just make sure you've finished it by next week, girls," she said in a cross voice. Then, she clapped her hands to the rest of the class to tell everyone to come and sit down at the front.

"Now," she began briskly when everyone was quite still, "you remember that the title of the show is *Shades of Nature*, but can anyone tell me which aspect of nature has not yet been mentioned?"

We all frowned hard.

"Fish?" asked Isobel after a moment.

Miss Coralie shook her head. I heard Tamsyn snigger.

"Is it the air?" asked Immy.

"No, but that's a clever thought. I'll tell you…"

And, right at that moment, something flashed into my mind. "Is it human beings?"

"Yes, Jasmine. Human beings. People. Being born and growing up. Now, I've choreographed a dance to some music that our clever pianist, Mrs. Marsden, has written herself…" We all looked at Mrs. Marsden. She seemed a bit embarrassed, as though she wasn't expecting Miss Coralie to say her name at that moment. "I've called it *Life*. This is going to be a dance for pupils of all ages. I'm picking one person to represent each class and the dance will form the *finale* of the show."

Every single one of us sat up a bit straighter at that moment. I saw a look go between Miss Coralie and Mrs. Marsden. It was a grown-up look. There are lots of those between Maman and Papa. And thinking that thought made my tummy quiver horribly, because I so wanted to be chosen for the *Life* dance, but it was sure to mean extra rehearsals and I knew that I'd never be allowed.

"My choreography for the *Life* dance is full of little cameo pictures. Like this..." Miss Coralie began to move and the silence seemed to grow another layer. Very slowly, she lifted her arms and uncurled her fingers. The movement was gentler than steam rising. Then, keeping perfect balance, she rose on tiptoe and spun around twice with her skirt swirling after her. It reminded me of a walnut whip. Her arms had floated high above her head but when she stopped turning they sank down into praying hands.

I went into a sort of dream imagining what the rest of the dance would look like, but then I came straight back to earth with a bang because Miss Coralie had suddenly changed back to her brisk self, and it was just as though she'd never said a word about the new dance.

"Right everybody, in your lines for the *révérence* please."

"We all hurried into place on tiptoe, and were just about to start the curtsey when Miss Coralie suddenly said, "Jasmine, can you see me afterwards?"

"Does that mean that you've chosen Jasmine?" Tamsyn asked in not such a loud voice as usual.

"I haven't decided yet," came the answer.

My heart banged against my ribs. Did she want to see me for a completely different reason? Was it because she was cross about our dance not being ready?

The moment the *révérence* music had finished, everyone started filing out. I could see Tamsyn out of the corner of my eye as I went to the front. She was hanging about because she wanted to hear what Miss Coralie was going to say. But Miss Coralie was talking to Mrs. Marsden and, by the time she'd finished, everyone else had gone out, so Tamsyn had to go too.

A flood of nervousness came over me when I saw Miss Coralie's serious face. I stood quite still except for my shivery legs.

"Jasmine," she began, "I had you in mind to represent this class in the *Life* dance..." An enormous *yessss* began to fill up my body, but seeped away faster than a balloon popping with her next words. "There are two things concerning me... Firstly, I don't want to overload you with extra practice, because you obviously still have a fair amount to do on your *Star* dance and, secondly, I'll need to have a word with your parents about the extra rehearsals for the *Life* dance. They'll be on Thursdays at 4.15. It's very important to attend, so if you're unable to manage these rehearsals, I'll need to know as soon as possible so that I can organize someone else in your place."

The shivers from my legs pushed their way

right round my body. "Did you say that *you'll* phone my parents, Miss Coralie?"

"Yes, certainly."

I nodded. I couldn't speak. My mind was racing away. It was good that Miss Coralie was going to be the one to speak to Maman and Papa. If *I'd* asked, Papa would just say that Thursday was my piano-lesson day and that was that.

"Er...how many extra rehearsals will there be?"

"Three or four... And nearer the time, when we start to put the whole thing together, you'd be needed for longer because of the show being in two sections." Miss Coralie was looking at me carefully. "I'll phone this evening then, Jasmine?"

I nodded again. Her eyes seemed to be locked into mine and I wondered if she could tell that I didn't think it would be any use. Papa would never let me do it, and sometimes I hated him for not letting me do what I loved most.

5 Talking in the Dark

"What is wrong, Jasmeen?"

We were going home in the car and I was hunched in the passenger seat with my arms folded. My sadness had turned to crossness.

"It's not fair."

"What's not fair?"

"I've been picked to be in the most important, most special part of the whole show and there's only one person from each class and I won't be allowed to do it because of stupid old Pa..." I couldn't say the truth, because it would have made my mum angry.

"...because of stupid old piano lessons."

"Why piano?"

"Because the extra rehearsals are on Thursdays."

Maman didn't say anything. We both knew that it was really Papa stopping me, because he was the one who decided whether I had to do piano lessons or not.

I wanted to make Maman suffer for being on Papa's side, not mine. "Miss Coralie's going to phone tonight, but there's no point, is there?"

"Well, we can't just expect Mrs. Waghorn to let you miss a chunk of the term every time there's something else going on in your life. She made it very clear when you started piano that learning any instrument is a commitment."

"But I didn't even want to learn."

Maman made a sort of snorty noise. "That's not how I remember it. You were begging to learn the piano."

"But that was before I realized how much I love ballet."

Maman set her lips in a tight thin line and stared at the road as though she was driving in a race.

I wriggled round inside my seat belt till I was facing her, knowing that I was acting like a baby. "Can't you make Papa say it's all right for me to go to one teensy little extra rehearsal every week. Pleeeeease?"

I did praying hands, but Maman had her eyes on the road, so she didn't even see.

"He let you do extra lessons last term for your exam."

A spurt of hope came over me. "So you think he'd let me do it again, then?"

She laughed a tinkly laugh. "No, *chérie*. What I mean is, you can't *keep* asking him for extra this and extra that."

The spurt of hope got squashed as I harrumphed myself back to facing the front and folded my arms even tighter than before. Now I was really acting like a baby. But I couldn't help it. "It's not fair."

When we got home, I tried again. Mum was making the tea and humming at the same time, except that I kept interrupting the humming.

"What time's he coming home, anyway?"

"Do you mean your father?"

"Yes!"

I couldn't help snapping because it was obvious I meant Papa, but I straight away wished I hadn't because Maman gave me a quick look with her eyebrows raised and the rest of her face set hard. I hate it when she does that. It's like a telling off without any words, which is worse than an ordinary telling off. She must have really had enough of me.

"What time's Papa coming home?" I tried again in a quiet voice.

"He may be late. And he will be tired."

I was used to Papa being tired. As well as

being a doctor, he also does operations. That's when he gets the most tired and comes home with his eyelids drooping right down.

"What if you tell him that this is the very last time I'll ever *ever* ask for extra rehearsals?"

"That's what I said last term. How many sausages?"

My crossness came back. "I don't know…it doesn't matter, does it?"

Out of the corner of my eye, I could see Maman getting her face ready to wear that mask look. She was standing perfectly still with the spatula in her hand. I thought I'd better give her a proper answer. "Two, please."

When the phone rang later on, I sat with my thumbs pressed against each other, and a little prayer going on inside my head as Maman answered it.

"Hello, Miss Coralie… Yes, Jasmine's told me." I wished I could hear what Miss Coralie was saying on the other end. Maman's face wasn't giving me any clues. She just kept nodding and saying, "I see." Eventually, she said, "Well, I'll have to talk to my husband, but the trouble is that Jasmine has piano lessons on a Thursday."

I held my breath and waited to see what she'd say next. It seemed like a very long wait. "Yes, yes, of course. I'll let you know tomorrow... All right... Thank you very much. Goodbye."

I gave Maman a fierce look but didn't speak. There was nothing to say.

"It's not the end of the world, Jasmeen. You're still going to be dancing with Poppy and that's very special, isn't it?"

Not as special as doing the Life *dance*, I thought, but what I said was, "Can you ask Papa tonight?"

"Yes, of course. Then I'll phone Miss Coralie tomorrow."

It was really difficult making my eyes stay open

as I lay in bed listening for the sound of Papa's key in the lock. I knew he was going to be late, but I never thought he'd be *this* late. I'd left my night-light on and I could see that the time on my Nutcracker Clock was twenty-five past ten. Maybe I'd better give in and go to sleep. It was just that Maman had promised to ask him about the rehearsals when he got in. My plan was to sneak out onto the stairs to listen.

I must have been practically asleep, because I suddenly jumped at the sound of the front door closing. In a flash, I was sitting upright with staring eyes, listening with all my might. It was silly. I knew that really. She wouldn't say anything the moment he walked through the door, would she? But...

Creak! That was the next-to-top stair. Oh, no! What if it was Papa? What if he popped his head round my door? I knew they both often did that. As fast as I'd shot up, I crashed back down again, snapping my eyes shut, pretending to be asleep. But lying all stiff and straight like a dead person, it was impossible. I could feel my eyes twitching because they were screwed up a bit too tightly.

"Jasmine, I can see perfectly well that you're awake." His voice was low.

My heart was really beating as I opened my eyes and sat up slowly, saying the first words that came into my head. "I couldn't get to sleep, Papa..."

He looked a bit sorry for me, and that made me carry on. "You see, I was worrying...about Miss Coralie..."

The very second the words were out of my mouth, I wished I could rub them out. But I had to carry on now.

"The trouble is, she really really wants me to have a special part in her show..."

"I know, Jasmine. We've been through this once. I'm going to do my best to make it, remember? It's the twenty-seventh, isn't it?" His voice sounded gentle and kind. And now he was smiling in a tired sort of way. But he obviously didn't realize that we were talking about different things. He was in such a good mood that I just couldn't help carrying on.

"Miss Coralie's chosen me out of the whole class to dance in the *finale* dance. There's only one of us from each class and she's made up the choreography herself. There are just a few extra rehearsals on...Thursdays." I broke into a gabble so that the *Thursday* word didn't stand out too much. "I told Miss Coralie that I was sure you wouldn't mind as it is so important..."

"A few?"

He didn't sound so soft and tired now.

"Three or four... And the full rehearsals might be a bit longer." I held my breath.

Papa sighed. "It's far too late to be having this kind of conversation now, Jasmine. You need to get to sleep or you'll be in no fit state to concentrate at school tomorrow." As he pulled the door to behind him, it felt as though a light had gone out inside my head. He hadn't exactly said no, but I can always tell when he's on his way to a no. Tears were tickling the sides of my face. I never knew they could squeeze themselves out of closed eyes.

6 Extraterrestrial Nutcrackers

"Hey, that's so cool!" It was Saturday afternoon. Rose was lying on her tummy on my bed. Poppy and I had just showed her the finished dance with the music. "You're really talented," she added, jumping up. Then she suddenly put on a totally posh, over-the-top voice. "But not as talented as me!" It was obvious that she was pretending to be Tamsyn. "Now *I'm* the only one in the class to be doing the *Life* dance. Goody goody. That means the audience will be looking at *me* more than ever!"

We both giggled. "You sound just like her," I said.

Rose sat on the floor. "Don't you mind not being in the *Life* dance, Jazz?"

I sighed. "Not any more... You see, I knew I'd never be allowed."

That wasn't totally true. Sometimes, on my own, I feel completely miserable about it. At other times I feel really mad, especially when I think of how Papa went off early the next morning after he'd talked to me that night. So it had been Maman who'd told me that I wasn't allowed. Maman phoned Miss Coralie and, the next lesson, we heard that Tamsyn had been chosen. But mostly I'm over it now. And I'm excited about our *Starshine* dance. I get such a wonderful feeling every time we rehearse it.

Rose was narrowing her eyes and clenching her fists. "Well, if I were you, I'd be so mad I'd have to chuck things round the room and scream the place down. When I see your dad I'm going to tell him off – big time."

"You'd better not, or you'll never be allowed in this house again," said Poppy, looking worried.

Rose didn't reply. She'd spotted one of my books on the book shelf and was pulling it out. At first I thought she was going to hurl it out of my bedroom window but instead she started flicking through the pages. But a moment later she was really glued to it. "Hey, this is saying all the reasons why ballet's supposed to be so good for you," she said, looking up. "You ought to show your dad this, you know, Jazz?"

I sighed. "There's no point. You can't argue with him. He always thinks he knows best."

"But what about all these things it says here?" Rose stabbed the book with her finger. "Stamina, strength, suppleness, coordination, balance, posture, concentration, aural skills, memory, confidence, creative skills and general awareness. I'm sure your dad would change his mind if he knew all that, Jazz."

"He wouldn't. Honestly. He thinks SATs are more important than that whole list."

"Well, anyway..." Rose suddenly started squirming around. "I'm going to the loo."

The moment she'd gone out, Poppy turned to me. "Where *is* your dad?"

"It's okay, he's at the gym."

"Phew! I'm just so scared that Rose'll say something and..."

But Poppy never finished the sentence because we both clearly heard Papa's voice downstairs.

I froze. "Oh no! He's back already!" Then I shot out of my room to try and grab Rose before she could say anything.

Uh-oh! Too late. As I leaned over the landing banister, I saw Rose standing in the hall with Papa. Poppy was at my side in a flash. She clapped her hand to her mouth to stop any squeaks coming out and we both hung there, watching and listening, with our hearts hammering away.

"Hello, Doctor Ayed."

I nearly gasped out loud. Rose was smiling and sticking her hand out.

Papa looked very puzzled as he shook her hand. "And you are...?"

"Rose Bedford. Jazz's friend." Then she pointed to the photo hanging up behind Papa. "Wow! You were really handsome when you were young, weren't you?"

"Well, I..." said Papa. I'd never heard him sound as though he didn't know what to say next.

"And you don't look at all like a scary person either."

This time I really did gasp.

"I...er..."

Rose didn't wait for an answer, just carried on talking. "It doesn't matter. I was just wondering why you didn't let Jazz do the extra rehearsals for the *Life* dance. She's really sad, you know."

Poppy drew up close to me. I could feel her arm all trembly and I knew mine would be the same.

Papa's eyes lost their puzzled look and he spoke quickly, as though he wasn't interested in the conversation any more. "Jasmine learns piano... She can't do everything." Then he started to walk away.

"But ballet's the most important thing in her whole life, Doctor Ayed."

Poppy clutched my trembly arm. Papa stopped walking and turned around. He looked at Rose with a sort of half-smile and spoke in a patient voice, as though she was a bit stupid. "Look, I really don't think it's any of your business, Rose."

"She doesn't look at all scared," Poppy whispered right into my ear.

I didn't reply. I was too busy listening to Rose. And I couldn't believe my ears. "Well, actually it *is* a bit, Doctor Ayed, because Jazz is my friend."

Poppy and I both gasped. Rose had really done it now.

Papa flicked his head sharply. I saw his eyes flash. Rose didn't seem to notice. She just kept talking away in her chirpy voice.

"And another thing... You see, I was reading this book all about ballet. And it said that ballet can really help you with things like school work and *especially* SATs."

I gulped and felt Poppy's shoulders going up. We looked at each other in alarm. Poppy's face was very pale and her freckles really stood out.

Rose was holding up the thumb of her left hand ready to start ticking off the list. "This is what ballet's good for, in case you didn't know...coordination, memory, concentration, posture..." She was reeling off all the words from the book. It was incredible that she'd remembered them so well. "...aural awareness, stamina, strength, suppleness, balance...er... confidence, creative skills, general awareness..."

Papa was staring at the carpet. I think he was waiting till Rose had definitely finished before he went mad.

I held my breath. Rose was silent. No wonder. She'd come to the end of the list.

But then, a second later, she was ticking her fingers off again as she came out with more words. Only she was just saying the first things that came into her head. "*Assemblé, pirouette, arabesque*, poltergeist, *chassé plié, perspiration...*"

I looked at Papa. His head had dropped right onto his chest. Rose was going to get a rocket. And whatever was she saying now?

"...energy, *révérence, pas de chat*, expression, *battement tendu*, adjective and extraterrestrial nutcrackers."

"What?" I squeaked, clutching Poppy and waiting for the big thunderclap to come.

Then I got the shock of my life because Papa's head came up and I could see tears swimming about in his eyes. He seemed to be shaking. What was happening? Surely Rose hadn't managed to make him feel ashamed of himself, had she? I grabbed Poppy's hand and pulled her downstairs. But, as we reached the bottom stair, Papa collapsed against the wall and let out a noise that reminded me of a happy chimpanzee I'd once seen on television. And that was when I realized that *my dad* was laughing. He was actually laughing his head off.

Rose broke into a massive grin. "So you never did change into a scary person, after all. You're just pretending, aren't you?"

Papa shook his head at Rose. "You...are ...incredible!" he spluttered through his big chuckles.

Then Maman appeared from the kitchen

looking completely puzzled, with a tea towel in her hands. "What's so funny?"

Papa turned to her and pointed at Rose. "This girl ought to be on the stage!"

Rose looked puzzled. "I'm not really much good at ballet..."

"Ballet? No, no, no. Being funny. Stand-up comic!" He looked at Maman again. "She's something else, this girl! You should have heard her!"

Rose eyed Papa suspiciously. "So...you're not sorry about not letting Jazz do the extra rehearsals?"

Papa didn't seem to hear her. He just did one more little chuckle. "Extraterrestrial nutcrackers indeed!"

Maman started giggling.

I looked at Rose. All the braveness seemed to have gone out of her. I suddenly felt really cross with Papa for laughing like that when all Rose had been trying to do was to help me, and he was just ignoring what she'd said completely. I went over to her and put my arm round her. "Come on, Rose. Let's go back up." As we turned, I made sure that I spoke in no more than a whisper. "Thank you for trying."

When we were halfway upstairs, she suddenly pulled away from me and her chin went up. "Never mind, Jazz, your dad might be able to stop you doing extra rehearsals, but he can never stop you loving ballet, can he?"

I turned round to see if Papa had heard. He had his hand on the kitchen door and Maman was saying something to him, so I didn't think he could have done. But when we got to the top I looked down and got a surprise. Papa's hand was still on the kitchen door and he was staring at the wall in a kind of trance. Then he turned to Maman and said, "Out of the mouths of babes."

I'd no idea what he meant, but it didn't matter anyway. Papa still thought he knew best, so there was no point in talking about it. There wasn't even any point in him coming to the show really. Nothing would change his mind. Nothing.

7 The Big Day

As the day of the show drew nearer and nearer, Poppy, Rose and I grew more and more excited and nervous. And there was another reason to be excited now, as well. Miss Coralie had told us that she'd arranged for a lady called Miss Bird to come and adjudicate at the show. Apparently, Miss Bird is an examiner and used to be a proper professional dancer when she was young. At the end of the show she was going to give out three special awards.

Tamsyn's hand had shot up straight away. "Will they be individual awards, Miss Coralie?"

"I've left that up to Miss Bird, but I should imagine so, yes. She'll be considering performance quality, technique and, in the case of the Tuesday students, choreography too."

I suddenly thought back to the lesson when Miss Coralie had watched Poppy and me do our dance together all through with the music for the first time. We hadn't danced our best because we'd both been feeling nervous, but I'd been able to tell from the look in Miss Coralie's eyes that she'd really liked it. She'd stayed completely silent at the end for ages, and then spoken with her breath more than her voice. "That was quite beautiful."

I'd felt a big lump in my throat when she'd said that and ever since I hadn't cared half so much about not being in the *Life* dance. I'd just practised and practised *Starshine* until I thought I couldn't dance it any better. Tamsyn had told us in the changing room that in one of the rehearsals for the *Life* dance, Miss Coralie had made her show all the other girls how to do one particular bit. That was the only time I felt a bit jealous because that might have been me. But then I quickly shook the stupid jealous thoughts away. Tamsyn might have been a show off, but she was also a brilliant dancer. Everyone was sure that she was going to get one of Miss Bird's merit awards.

Papa had never said anything to me about Rose, but I'd asked Maman the meaning of "Out of the mouths of babes" because I couldn't get those words out of my head. She'd said it was an expression which meant that sometimes children – even very young children – happen to hit on a simple truth, where adults haven't been able to. Once or twice, I'd wondered what that simple truth might be, but most of the time I was too excited and nervous about the show to think about anything else. And whether or not Papa would be there, was sitting right at the top of my thoughts.

Eventually the day came.

"This is really really it! I can't believe it!" said Poppy, clutching my hands.

We were waiting in the line to have our make-up put on. Our costumes were absolutely beautiful. Both of us were wearing deep-blue, sleeveless leotards with a glittery silver edge to the neck and matching elastic belts. From the belts floated strips of silky, silvery-blue ribbons. Our ballet shoes were black. Our hair was scraped right back and we both wore tiny sparkling coronets.

"Smile for the camera!" said Lottie, who was going round taking everyone's picture.

Poppy and I put our arms round each other and our heads together for the photo. When she'd taken it, Lottie said, "You two look beautiful, you know, especially because of Jasmine being so dark and Poppy being so pale."

Poppy and I didn't know what to say, so we just kept smiling and when Lottie had gone we did a thumb-thumb. I'd lost count of the number of times we'd done that in the last hour while we'd been in here getting ready and warming up. It was partly for good luck in our dance, but also partly because we were hoping that my dad would be there. Maman had come on her own and said that Papa would be joining her just as soon as he got back from his conference.

The changing room was really the small hall in the Community Centre, but it was just the right size for all the Tuesday girls, all the little ones and a few older ones. The students who were fourteen or more were upstairs in a sort of cloakroom because there weren't many of them.

The younger ones were already changed, with their make-up on, because they were the first to go on stage. They'd been collected by Miss Eleanor and Miss Melissa, who are the other two teachers at Miss Coralie's, and taken to wait in the wings. I expect some of them were already in their positions on the stage behind the big heavy velvet curtain. Just thinking that thought made a swarm of butterflies come whizzing into my stomach.

Rose was on the other side of the room running through her dance with the other two girls in her group. As soon as Poppy and I had our make-up on, we went through the first bit of our own dance.

"Your knee's not stretched on that *rond de jambe*, Poppy," said Tamsyn, going past us at that moment.

Poppy went a bit red. I wanted to tell Tamsyn to mind her own business, but I didn't dare. Anyway, Miss Coralie had come into the room.

"Right, everybody." She clapped her hands. "All eyes on me, please." She didn't really have to say it. We were already silent, waiting to hear what was happening. "The show begins in less than five minutes. From now on, we talk only in whispers, because loud talking in here will be heard from the audience. I've had a peep through the curtain and the hall is packed." Everyone nodded nervously. "Three minutes before you're needed, you'll be called by myself, Miss Melissa or Miss Eleanor. Immediately before you perform, take two or three slow deep breaths and focus hard on what you're about to do, then try to imagine you're growing wings and are about to fly across the world."

My heart grew inside my chest when Miss Coralie said those words. I knew exactly what she meant. I couldn't wait to be on the stage now. Absolutely couldn't wait.

8 Growing Wings and Flying

"On you go, Rose," said Miss Coralie. "Deep breath."

For once, Rose's footsteps didn't make a sound as she tiptoed to centre front stage. Poppy was in the opposite back wing from me. We gave each other shaky smiles then the heavy curtains slid slowly apart and Rose's voice rang out over the whole hall.

> *The sky is deep and dark.*
> *The sky is dark and deep.*
> *The world is still and silent.*
> *Everyone's asleep.*

Who is strong enough to drag
the heavy black away?
Or peel it, chip it, bit by bit
until it turns to day?

Glinting in the blackness is
a single twinkling star,
Trying to drizzle silver dust –
not getting very far.

"I need a friend to help me.
If we touch we'll make a flare of light!"
And so the star set off to search.
And search and search that lonely night.

This was it! The poem had finished. Rose was standing perfectly still, the audience were clapping and my heart was thumping. Somewhere out there in the darkness was Maman. And maybe Papa too. Maybe. I wouldn't know, because I couldn't look for him when I was dancing. Anyway, it would be too dark to see.

I took two slow deep breaths as I watched Rose walk off to the front wing. Then, as the music started, something magic made me rise onto my toes. It must have been magic because I don't remember telling myself to do it. I ran on tiptoe right across to the opposite front corner of the stage and sank to my knees, knowing without looking that Poppy would be doing the same thing, four beats later, from her side of the stage. And, from that moment on, I really felt as though I *was* a lonely star in the sky.

I wasn't nervous at all any more, just floaty and strong but light as a feather as I danced and danced, better than I'd ever danced before. And though I knew Poppy was there, she didn't seem like Poppy, she seemed like just another lonely star swirling and swooping in the deep, black night.

As the end of the music came with a string of glittering notes that floated into the air, we held our final positions in front centre stage. I was facing stage right and Poppy stage left. This was the most difficult part of all. My heart was really thumping from dancing with all my energy, but trying to make it look smooth and easy and liquid. And now we had to balance on our front foot and raise the back one in a low *arabesque*. There was so much to think about – turning out, not bending the supporting knee, pulling up out of your ribs, not rolling on your feet, keeping your alignment, not leaning forwards too much, pointing your toes, not lifting your shoulders, tilting your head to look out to the audience...

And then I couldn't resist it. I just had to look. My eyes flitted over the rows of people all smiling and clapping and clapping. I saw Maman straight away, but there was an empty seat beside her. My body felt suddenly drained. Papa hadn't made it. I let my *arabesque* drop and Poppy did the same because we'd agreed to hold it as long as we could and when the first one dropped it, the other one would do the same. Usually it was Poppy who dropped first. But this time it was me. I just didn't have the heart to hold it for another second.

As we straightened up to do our curtsey, my eyes flitted to the back of the auditorium and there, standing up tall, with a proud smile on his face, was Papa. He met my eyes and gave me a double thumbs-up then started everyone off in another burst of applause. All my energy came flooding back and I wished I could do the whole dance again, and this time I'd hold the *arabesque* for ever. Papa had seen me and he was proud of me.

I sank into the curtsey at exactly the same moment as Poppy and then the curtains swished across in front of us.

9 The Awards

We were all sitting on the stage facing the audience. The show had finished and Miss Bird had come up onto the stage too. She'd been sitting in the third row right in the middle. Papa was in the seat beside Maman now. I'd given them both a little wave and then started concentrating on Miss Bird.

"I knew that would be the adjudicator," Tamsyn whispered into the back of my neck. "I spotted her right away, you know."

I didn't turn round because Miss Bird was about to start talking. She was half facing us and half facing the audience, so she could talk to everyone at once.

"Ssh!" said Rose.

But Tamsyn didn't *ssh*. "Can I squeeze in next to you lot?" she said. "I can't see properly from back here."

It hadn't been a squash when we were standing, but everyone took up more room when they were sitting down. Tamsyn pushed in between me and Lottie. She was kneeling up very straight, blocking the view of the girls behind her.

Miss Bird welcomed the audience and said it was a privilege to be the adjudicator. She talked about the new hall and the lovely stage and how we'd all made it seem like a proper theatre because of our lovely dancing. Then she said she was going to announce who had won the three special merit awards.

"I had a very difficult time trying to select just three people, and I found it virtually impossible to pick out individuals from the smaller groups, particularly in the case of groups working closely together. My first award is a most appropriate one, because the three little girls concerned performed a dance that must have been specially for me..." She broke into a big smile. "*The Dance of the Birds!* So well done to Milly Landon, Phoebe Wright and Rachel Warder!"

We all burst into applause as Milly, Rachel and Phoebe got up and went over to Miss Bird. Miss Coralie must have told the little ones to curtsey if they won an award, because all three girls did sweet curtseys. I heard some ladies in the audience say "Aaah!"

"But that's just one award, isn't it?" hissed Tamsyn right in my ear. "There are still two more to come, aren't there?"

I didn't even look at her, just nodded. She'd already stopped clapping and was kneeling even straighter.

"My second award is for an individual," said Miss Bird. "This is a girl who I'm quite sure will go far. I want you to remember her name because I think one day we'll see it in lights." Miss Bird left a big long pause before she said the name.

"Bet it's Katie," Poppy whispered to me.

"Or Tamsyn," I whispered back.

"Katie Denver, please come and receive your award."

A big cheer went up as Katie stood up slowly. She's fourteen but she's quite shy and you could see she was a bit embarrassed because she looked down at the stage as she walked to Miss Bird. I was clapping so much my hands were hurting, but Tamsyn was hardly clapping at all. I think she wanted to get on with the last award.

Katie shook hands and did a tiny little bob curtsey. She looked so graceful. I agreed with Miss Bird. One day Katie would be a real ballerina. When I saw her dancing, I thought there was probably no hope in the world for my ballerina dream to come true.

"And my last award is also for a group," Miss Bird was saying.

"A group? She's not going to give the award to *everyone* in the *Life* dance, surely!" said Tamsyn, in a heavy whisper.

"Ssh!" hissed Rose.

"A very talented group indeed." She looked round all of us and her eyes seemed to have settled on Tamsyn. But then she must have been saying the wrong words. "And a very small group! Well done to Poppy Vernon and Jasmine Ayed."

I gasped.

"Huh!" said Tamsyn, only it came out like a snort.

I couldn't move! I just sat there in a trance. It couldn't be us. What about Tamsyn?

But Poppy was already on her feet. "Come on," she whispered. Her cheeks were bright pink.

"It's us!"

"Go on, Jazz!" said Rose, patting me on the back really hard. "You brilliant things!"

Poppy and I walked over to Miss Bird and shook hands like Katie had done, then did the same bob curtsey as the audience started clapping.

Miss Bird looked tiny from close-up. She was only a bit taller than me and she'd got high heels on as well. Her cheek bones were huge and pointy. I couldn't stop staring at them. Her face was like a heart with two dark eyes in the middle. Her eyelashes were thick and curly.

"Congratulations, my dears," she whispered to us. "And did you make up the poem too?"

"Poppy did," I said.

"Quite beautiful. I'd like a copy of that, if I may."

We nodded even harder. And smiled and smiled. This really *was* like a ballerina dream come true.

10 Me and My Dad

When Poppy, Rose and I had got changed, we went across the stage and down the front steps to find our parents. It felt strange going through the curtain and seeing no audience. All the chairs had been moved to the sides and everyone was standing around talking.

I spotted Maman right away, talking with Poppy and Rose's mums, but I couldn't see Papa. Then Poppy nudged me and, when I followed her gaze, I saw that he was standing on his own at the side looking at the programme.

"See you in a minute, Poppy."

I felt a bit shy going over to him for some reason, but the shyness disappeared when he gave me a massive smile.

"Did you see me do the whole dance?"

"Well, I'm not sure..." I felt a jab of disappointment. "I think it might have been someone else I was watching actually... Someone from the Royal Ballet School!" He gave me a wink and pointed to his programme. "Though it does say Jasmine Ayed here, so I guess it must have been you."

Happiness sizzled through my whole body. Papa had *really* thought I was good.

"Clever girl," he said, kissing the top of my head. "I'm very proud of you."

And that's when Maman came over with Poppy and Rose and their mums. A moment later, Miss Bird joined us too.

She crinkled into a smile and started telling us about four tickets that she'd been sent by her daughter to go and see her dancing in a ballet called *Rhonda*, at Sadler's Wells.

"I was going to ask my other daughter to come along with her husband and their little girl," said Miss Bird. "But, of course, they've seen Anna dancing many many times, so it's not such a treat for them..."

I couldn't help interrupting, I just had to know... "It's not Anna Lane, is it?"

Miss Bird broke into a big beaming smile. "Yes, it is. So you've heard of my daughter!"

Poppy and I turned very slowly towards each other and, if my eyes looked as big as hers at that moment, they must have looked absolutely massive.

"So, I was wondering if you three might like to come and see the ballet with me. I'm sure Anna would be delighted to give you a guided tour backstage afterwards. It's on the nineteenth of next month."

Everyone started thanking Miss Bird like mad. But Papa was looking at Maman with a frown on his face. "Isn't that the weekend your mother invited us all to Paris?"

I knew there'd be something. There always was. I hung my head, feeling a terrible sadness gathering round me.

"So does that mean I can't go?" I asked in a small voice.

"I'm afraid..." Papa began, then he suddenly broke off and looked at Rose. She was staring at him hard. He narrowed his eyes, as though he was remembering something, then looked back at me.

"I think we can explain to Mami that something rather special has come up and see if we can't rearrange things."

Rose and Poppy and I all looked at each other, eyes wide.

"You mean...I can go?" I dared to ask.

Papa nodded. He was giving me a special smile.

"You must be very proud of Jasmine," said

Miss Bird. "Such a talented girl, both at dancing and choreography." She patted Papa's hand as though he was a little boy. "She's going to go far, I know."

The three mums had gone off into their own conversation by now. Poppy, Rose and I were looking at the silver shield that Poppy and I had won. Papa was looking at the floor and, even though his voice was scarcely more than a whisper, I could just about hear what he was saying to Miss Bird.

"I had it pointed out to me recently that if someone loves something more than anything in the world, there's absolutely nothing anyone can do to stop that love. I was very struck by those words." Rose and I looked at each other, open-mouthed. "And then this afternoon, standing at the back of the audience, I realized something else. If someone loves something as much as all that, why would anyone *want* to try and stop them loving it?"

"Wise words, Mr Ayed," said Miss Bird, patting Papa's arm again.

"Er...*Doctor* Ayed, actually," said Rose, stepping forward.

"Oh, I'm sorry..." began Miss Bird.

"Not at all," said Papa.

Then his arm reached out for me, so I snuggled into him and he squeezed my shoulder.

I felt like dancing round the whole hall singing at the top of my voice, but I didn't want to move from where I was. So I just smiled at my two friends and they both came closer to me. That meant we could do our thumb-thumb. Only this time it wasn't for luck, it was for *yesssssssssssssssss*!

Basic Ballet Positions

First position

Second position

Third position

Fourth position

Fifth position

Ballet words are mostly in French, which makes them more magical. But when you're learning, it's nice to know what they mean too. Here are some of the words that all Miss Coralie's students have to learn:

adage The name for the slow steps in the centre of the room, away from the *barre*.

arabesque A beautiful balance on one leg.

assemblé A jump where the feet come together at the end.

battement dégagé A foot exercise at the *barre* to get beautiful toes.

battement tendu Another foot exercise where you stretch your foot until it points.

chassé A soft smooth slide of the feet.

echappé This one's impossible to describe, but it's like your feet escaping from each other!

fifth position croisé When you are facing, say the *left* corner, with your feet in fifth position, and your front foot is the *right* foot.

fouetté This step is so fast your feet are in a blur! You do it to prepare for *pirouettes*.

grand battement High kick!

jeté A spring where you land on the opposite foot. Rose loves these!

pas de bourrée Tiny little steps to the side, like a mouse.

pas de chat A cat hop from one foot to the other.

plié This is the first step we do in class. You have to bend your knees slowly and make sure your feet are turned right out, with your heels firmly planted on the floor for as long as possible.

port de bras Arm movements, which Poppy
is good at.

révérence The curtsey at the end of class.

rond de jambe This is where you make a
circle with your leg.

sissonne A scissor step.

sissonne en arrière A scissor step going backwards.
This is really hard!

sissonne en avant A scissor step going forwards.

soubresaut A jump off two feet, pointing your feet hard
in the air.

temps levé A step and sweep up the other leg then jump.

turnout You have to stand with your legs and feet and
hips all opened out and pointing to the side, not the front.
This is the most important thing in ballet that everyone
learns right from the start.